a Little Golden Book® Collection

Inspirational Tales

A GOLDEN BOOK • NEW YORK

Contents

Where Do Kisses Come From?

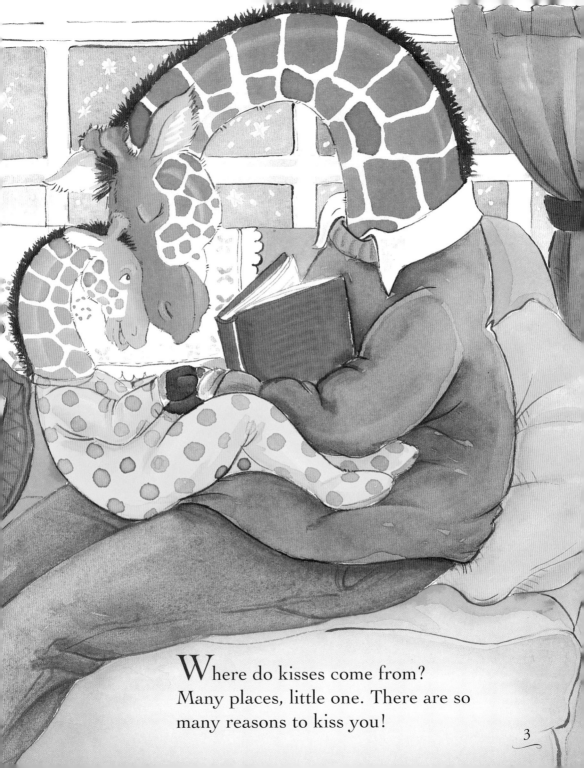

Where do kisses come from?
Many places, little one. There are so
many reasons to kiss you!

3

Kisses come from the way your eyes shine like
two suns when you open them in the morning . . .

and from your smile, sweet as maple syrup.

Kisses come from the way you look
in your favorite hat.

They come from tummy tickles and other
silly giggly games.

Some kisses come from chocolate-covered noses.

Others come from skinned knees and scraped elbows.

Kisses come from your special way of helping.

And from the way you make up silly
songs while splashing in the tub.

Kisses come from the way you snuggle up for a story, your cheek as soft as a rose petal.

Kisses also come from wishes for
sweet, sweet dreams.

There are so many kinds
of kisses, little one.
I-missed-you kisses . . .

thank-you kisses . . .

feel-better kisses . . .

and kisses just because.

But no matter what kind of kiss it is,
ALL kisses come from love.

My Mommy always finds a way
to make me feel special every day.
Because she's fun and caring, too,
I love everything we do.

We sometimes go to the street fair
to see the neat attractions there.
Maybe we'll eat hotdogs on sticks
and see a magician doing tricks.

At the stadium we clap and cheer
for the baseball players every year.
Together we love to stand and shout,
"One! Two! Three strikes—you're out!"

When lightning comes and raindrops fall,
we stay indoors and have a ball.
We bake bread, then eat it warm,
and forget about the thunderstorm.

The museum I like best of all
is filled with dinosaurs big and tall.
Mommy takes me all around
to see the bones found in the ground.

DINO DIG!

Quiet time inside is nice.
We play a game—sometimes twice—
or make puppets from old socks
Mommy keeps in a homemade box.

Basketball is my favorite sport.
I shoot and dribble down the court.
Mom's the coach and she helps me
to be the best that I can be.

Everything we do and see
becomes a treasured memory.
I love you, Mommy, and this is true:
The greatest gift is a hug from you!

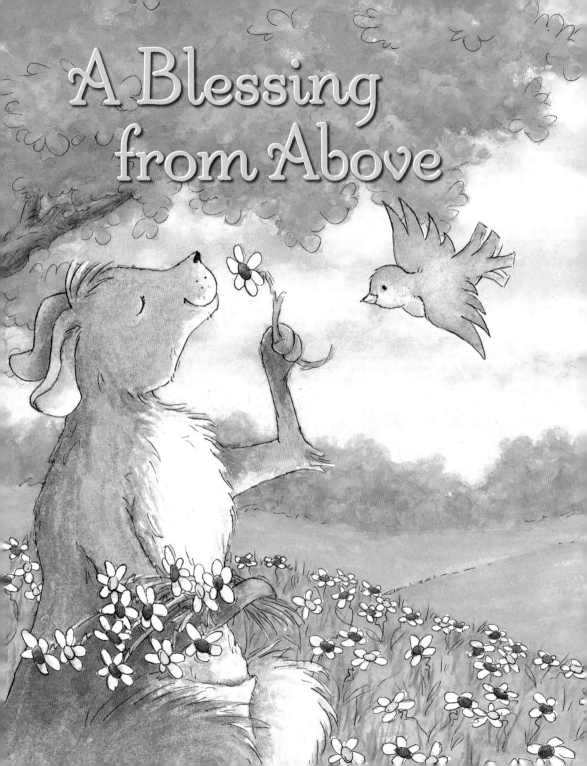

A Blessing from Above

Children are a gift from God; they are His reward.
—Psalm 127:5

Once upon a time there lived a mother kangaroo who had an empty pouch.

Every night before she went to sleep, she prayed that someday her pouch would be filled with a baby to love and hold and care for.

One day, Momma-Roo went for a walk.

Along the way, she saw a pair of butterflies
fluttering about in a field of flowers.

She later came upon a mother duck leading her
ducklings to a pond.

Next she spied a mama and papa squirrel gathering acorns for their family.

She looked forward to the day she could share
such wonderful sights and activities with a baby of
her own.

Momma-Roo was getting tired. She
decided to rest underneath the branches
of a beautiful willow tree.

When she looked up she saw a bluebird
nest stuffed full of baby bluebird eggs.

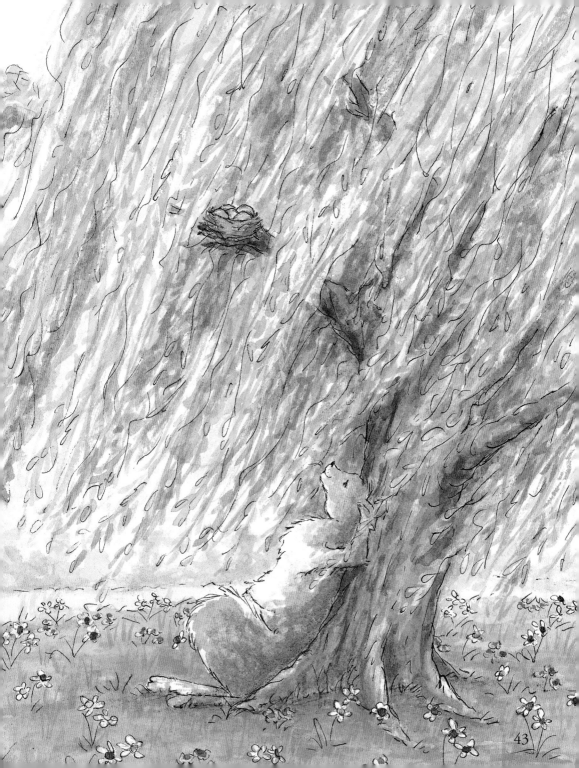

One by one, the eggs began to hatch.
The baby bluebirds stretched their wings and cried
for food.

The nest was getting very crowded.

Just as the last and littlest bluebird cracked
open his shell and stepped into this world . . .

. . . one of his brothers stretched his wings for the first time.

Before the littlest one knew what was happening, he was bumped from the nest and falling . . .

down,

down,

down . . .

47

. . . straight into Momma-Roo's pouch!

The baby bluebird peeked out from the pouch
and gazed up at Momma-Roo.
"Hello, Mommy," he chirped.

The mother bluebird
looked down and saw her
littlest one.

She knew her nest
was not big enough for
all her chicks. It made
her happy to see her
baby in such a warm,
cuddly place.

"Hello, Little One," said Momma-Roo.

Then she hugged her blessing from above.
"At last! My very own baby!" she cried joyfully.
"I will cherish you and love you forever!"

On their way back home, Momma-Roo and Little One frolicked through the field of flowers.

They stopped for a sip of water at the pond.

They shared grass and berries with each other.
They were so happy!

Now, every night before they fall asleep,
Momma-Roo and Little One thank God for all
their blessings . . . but especially for each other.

In love He destined us
for adoption to Himself. . . .
—Ephesians 1:5

The Lion's Paw

Ow! roared the lion.
"There is a thorn in my paw.
Who will take it out?"

"Not I," said the solid rhinoceros.
"I am sharpening my pointed
horn."

"Not I," said the startled kudu.
"I am racing away from here!"

"Not I," whispered the tall
giraffe among the tip-top leaves.

"Not I," said the bouncing baboon.
"I am having too much fun."

"Who will take the thorn out?"
asked the crowned crane.

"Not I," said the hippopotamus.
"I am cooling off in the mud."

"Not I," said the striped zebra.
"I am kicking up my heels."

"Not I," said the bright-eyed monkey.
"I am swinging by my tail."

"Not I," said the big gorilla.
"I am scratching away my fleas."

"Not I," said the elegant gazelle.
"I am leaping across the veld."

"Will no one remove the thorn?"
called the ibis by the purple pool.

"Not I," said the slippery crocodile,
smiling a hungry smile.

"Not I," said the trumpeting elephant.
"I am taking a shower."

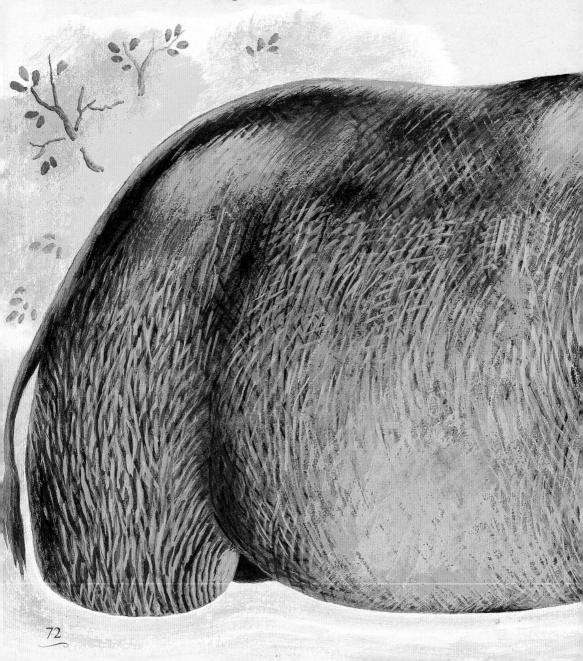

"Not I," said the spotted leopard.
"I am slinking through the shade."

"Not I," said the solemn buffalo.
"I have too much work to do."

"Who will help the lion?" cried the
ostrich running over the desert sands.

"Not I," said the sulky camel.
"I am chewing my chewy cud."

"Not I," said the swooping vulture.
"I'm busy hunting a meal."

"Not I," said the fast cheetah.
"I'm busy hunting, too."

"I will," said the little mouse.
And she did!

Daddy, I love you,
and I want you to know,
I have a great time
wherever we go.

At the carwash we pretend
we're deep in the sea,
and the brushes are fish
waving their fins at me.

85

Camping is my favorite
summer event.
We sleep in the woods—
I help pitch the tent!

We plant seeds out back
in neat, straight rows,
and then water them
with the garden hose.

Going to the petting zoo
is always lots of fun.
We feed goats, pigs, and sheep
out in the bright, warm sun.

When snow covers the ground
and the hills are all white,
we sled and make snowballs
from morning to night.

At the neighborhood park
we jump, swing, and play.
Soon the sun sets.
Have we been here all day?

I love you, Daddy,
for all that we do.
In a contest for best dad,
the winner is you!

PRAYERS
for Children

Acknowledgments

"A Great Gray Elephant" is reprinted with the permission of
Simon & Schuster from *The Child on His Knees* by Mary Dixon
Thayer. Copyright 1926 by Macmillan Publishing Company,
copyright renewed 1954 by Mary D. T. Fremont-Smith.

Dear Father,
Hear and Bless

Dear Father,
    hear and bless
Thy beasts
    and singing birds:
And guard
    with tenderness
Small things
    that have no words.

Morning Prayer

Now, before I run to play,
    Let me not forget to pray
To God Who kept me through the night
    And waked me with the morning light.

Help me, Lord, to love Thee more
    Than I ever loved before,
In my work and in my play,
    Be Thou with me through the day.
                Amen.

I Thank Thee, Lord

I thank Thee, Lord, for quiet rest,
    And for Thy care of me;
O let me through this day be blest
    And kept from harm by Thee.

—Mary L. Duncan

The Gift

What can I give Him,
   Poor as I am?
If I were a shepherd
   I would bring a lamb.
If I were a Wise Man
   I would do my part.
Yet what can I give Him?
   Give my heart.

—Christina Rossetti

Be present at our table, Lord,
Be here and everywhere adored.
These morsels bless, and grant that we
May feast in Paradise with Thee. Amen.

A Great Gray Elephant

A great gray elephant,
　　A little yellow bee,
　　A tiny purple violet,
　　　　A tall green tree,
A red and white sailboat
On a blue sea—
All these things
You gave to me,
When you made
My eyes to see—
　　　　Thank you, God!

He Prayeth Well, Who Loveth Well

He prayeth well,
   Who loveth well
Both man and bird and beast.
He prayeth best,
   Who loveth best
All things both great and small;
For the dear God
   Who loveth us,
He made and loveth all.

—Samuel Taylor Coleridge,
   from *The Rime of the Ancient Mariner*

Father, We Thank Thee

For flowers that bloom about our feet,
  Father, we thank Thee,
For tender grass so fresh and sweet,
  Father, we thank Thee,
For the song of bird and hum of bee,
For all things fair we hear or see,
Father in heaven, we thank Thee.

For blue of stream and blue of sky,
  Father, we thank Thee,
For pleasant shade of branches high,
  Father, we thank Thee,
For fragrant air and cooling breeze,
For beauty of the blooming trees,
Father in heaven, we thank Thee.

For this new morning with its light,
  Father, we thank Thee,
For rest and shelter of the night,
  Father, we thank Thee,
For health and food, for love and friends,
For everything Thy goodness sends,
Father in heaven, we thank Thee.

—Ralph Waldo Emerson

Evening Hymn

I hear no voice, I feel no touch,
I see no glory bright;
But yet I know that God is near,
In darkness as in light.
He watches ever by my side,
And hears my whispered prayer:
The Father for His little child
Both night and day doth care.

—Anonymous

Jesus, Tender Shepherd, Hear Me

Jesus, tender Shepherd, hear me;
Bless Thy little lamb tonight;
Through the darkness be Thou near me,
Watch my sleep till morning light.
All this day Thy hand has led me,
And I thank Thee for Thy care;
Thou has warmed and clothed and fed me;
Listen to my evening prayer.

—Mary L. Duncan

A Child's Prayer

God, make my life a little light
    Within the world to glow;
A little flame that burneth bright
    Wherever I may go.
God, make my life a little flower
    That giveth joy to all,
Content to bloom in native bower,
    Although the place be small.
God, make my life a little song
    That comforteth the sad,
That helpeth others to be strong
    And makes the singer glad.
God, make my life a little staff
    Whereon the weak may rest,
And so what health and strength I have
    May serve my neighbors best.
God, make my life a little hymn
    Of tenderness and praise;
Of faith, that never waxeth dim,
    In all His wondrous ways.

—M. Betham-Edwards

Jesus, from Thy Throne on High

Jesus, from Thy throne on high,
    Far above the bright blue sky,
Look on me with loving eye;
    Hear me, Holy Jesus.

Be Thou with me every day,
    In my work and in my play,
When I learn and when I pray;
    Hear me, Holy Jesus.

—Thomas B. Pollock

Good-Night Prayer

Father, unto Thee I pray,
Thou hast guarded me all day;
Safe I am while in Thy sight,
Safely let me sleep tonight.

Bless my friends, the whole world bless;
Help me to learn helpfulness;
Keep me ever in Thy sight;
So to all I say good night.

—Henry Johnstone

Bedtime Prayer

Now I lay me down to sleep,
I pray Thee, Lord, thy child to keep:
Thy love guard me through the night
And wake me with the morning light.

Amen.

Good Night

Good night! Good night! Far flies the light;
But still God's love shall flame above,
Making all bright. Good night! Good night!

God Watches Us

God watches o'er us all the day, at home, at school, and at our play;
And when the sun has left the skies, He watches with a million eyes.

—Gabriel Setoun

My Little Golden Book About
GOD

GOD IS GREAT.

Look at the stars in the evening sky,
so many millions of miles away
that the light you see shining left its star
long, long years before you were born.

Yet even beyond the farthest star,
God knows the way.
Think of the snow-capped mountain peaks.
Those peaks were crumbling away with
age before the first people lived on earth.
Yet when they were raised up sharp and new
God was there, too.

Bend down to touch the smallest flower.
Watch the busy ant tugging at his load.
See the flash of jewels on the insect's back.
This tiny world your two hands could span,
like the oceans and mountains and far-off stars,
God planned.

Think of our earth, spinning in space . . .

For GOD IS GOOD.

God gives us everything we need—
shelter from cold and wind and rain,
clothes to wear and food to eat.

God gives us flowers, the songs of birds,
the laughter of brooks, the deep song of the sea.

He sends the sunshine

to make things grow,

sends in its turn
the needed rain.

129

God makes us grow, too, with minds and eyes
to look about our wonderful world,
to see its beauty, to feel its might.

131

He gives us a small, still voice in our hearts
to help us tell wrong from right.
God gives us hopes and wishes and dreams,
plans for our grown-up years ahead.

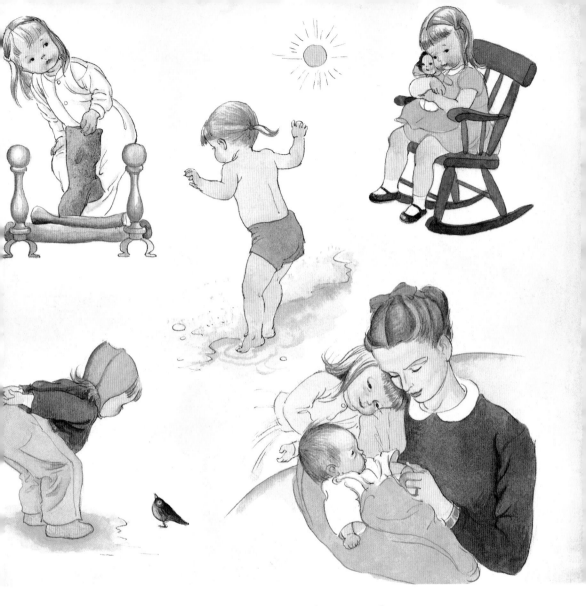

He gives us memories of yesterdays,
so that happy times and people we love
we can keep with us always in our hearts.
For GOD IS LOVE.

God is the love of our mother's kiss,

the warm, strong hug of our daddy's arms.

God is in all the love we feel
for playmates and family and friends.

When we're hurt or sorry or lonely or sad,
if we think of God, He is with us there.

God whispers to us in our hearts:
"Do not fear, I am here,
And I love you, my dear.
Close your eyes and sleep tight,
For tomorrow will be bright—
All is well, dear child.
Good night."

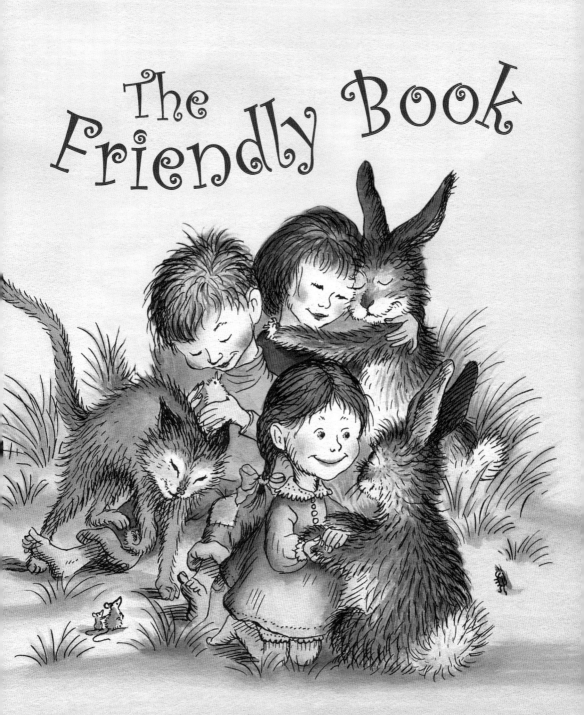

I LIKE CARS
Red cars   Green cars
Sport limousine cars
I like cars
A car in a garage
A car with a load
A car with a flat tire
A car on the road
I like cars.

I LIKE TRAINS
Express trains
Toy trains
Streamline trains
Freight trains
Old trains
Milk trains

Any kind of train
A train in the station
Trains crossing the plains

Trains in a snowstorm
Trains in the rain
I like trains.

144

I LIKE STARS
Yellow stars
Green stars
Red stars
Blue stars
I like stars
Far stars
Quiet stars
Bright stars
Light stars
I like stars

A star that is shooting across the dark sky
A star that is shining right straight in your eye
I like stars.

I LIKE SNOW
Cold snow
Slow snow
White snow
Icy snow
I like snow
Snow falling softly with everything still
White in the blue night, white on the sill
White on the trees on the far distant hill
With everything still
I like snow.

I LIKE SEEDS

Mustard seeds   Radish seeds
Corn seeds   Flower seeds
Any kind of seed
Seeds that are sprouting green from the ground
And seeds of the milkweed flying around
I like seeds.

I LIKE BUGS
Black bugs   Green bugs
Bad bugs   Mean bugs
Any kind of bug
A bug in a rug
A bug in the grass
A bug on the sidewalk
A bug in a glass
I like bugs
Round bugs   Shiny bugs
Fat bugs   Buggy bugs
Big bugs   Lady bugs
I like bugs.

I LIKE FISH
Silver fish   Gold fish
Black fish   Old fish
Young fish   Fishy fish
Any kind of fish

A fish in a pond
A fish in a stream
A fish in the ocean
A fish in a dream
I like fish.

153

I LIKE DOGS
Big dogs   Little dogs
Fat dogs   Doggy dogs
Old dogs   Puppy dogs

155

I like dogs
A dog that is barking over the hill
A dog that is dreaming very still
A dog that is running wherever he will
I like dogs.

I LIKE BOATS
Any kind of boat
Tug boats   Tow boats
Large boats   Barge boats

Sail boats   Whale boats
Thin boats   Skin boats
Rubber boats   River boats
Flat boats   Cat boats
U boats   New boats

Tooting boats   Hooting boats
South American fruit boats
Bum boats   Gun boats
Slow boats   Row boats
I like boats.

I LIKE WHISTLES

Wild whistles   Bird whistles
Far-off heard whistles
Boat whistles   Train whistles
I like whistles

The postman's whistle
The policeman's whistle
The wind that blows away the thistle
Light as the little birds whistle and sing
And the little boy whistling in the spring
The wind that whistles through the trees
And blows the boats across the seas
I like whistles.

I LIKE PEOPLE
Glad people
Sad people
Slow people
Mad people
Big people
Little people

I like people.

WONDERS
OF NATURE

Isn't it a wonder the way the woods know that spring is coming before the snow is gone?

The sleeping plants send up green shoots. And the tree buds swell and burst.

Isn't it a wonder
that some seeds
have wings . . .

ASH

ELM

MAPLE

MILKWEED

and some have
tiny silken
parachutes,

DANDELION

and some seeds
are hidden away
in fruits . . .

APPLE

CORN

BEAN

BEAN

and that every seed,
no matter how tiny,
has a whole tiny plant
inside, with food to use
when it starts to grow?

Isn't it a wonder
that under the sea
there are beautiful,
strange gardens
where the "flowers" are
animals?

SEA GRAPES

SEA ANEMONE

SEA LILY

SEA CUCUMBER

SEA URCHIN

SEA ANEMONE

Sea anemones, sea lilies,
sea cucumbers, and sea grapes—
all are animals!

SEA CUCUMBER

SEA ANEMONE

Isn't it a wonder
that tiny coral animals
under the sea,
which never move,
build great towers
and whole islands
of their tiny shells?

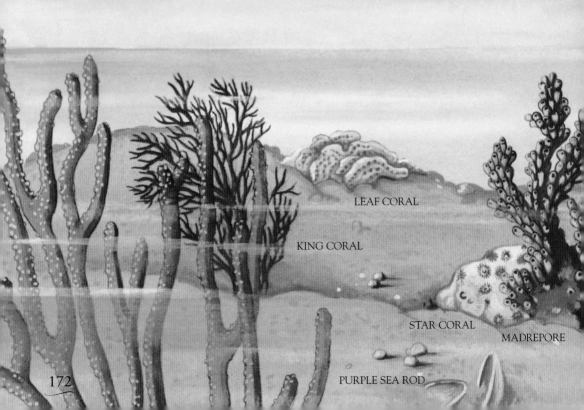

LEAF CORAL

KING CORAL

STAR CORAL

MADREPORE

PURPLE SEA ROD

ORGAN-PIPE
CORAL

BRAIN CORAL

CUP CORAL

Isn't it a wonder
that on the dry desert
some plants have thick stems
in which they store water . . .
and no leaves at all . . .
and lots of prickly spines
to keep thirsty animals
from eating them up?

And the kangaroo rat
who lives on the desert
never drinks water,
but makes it in its body
out of crisp, dry seeds.

Isn't it a wonder
that the beaver
can bite a young tree through
in just a few minutes?

He bites off the branches and uses them
to build a dam across a stream.

And all the birds around,
and the squirrels and opossums,
the deer and the moose,
enjoy that beaver pond.

Isn't it a wonder
that in the jungles
the leaves grow so thickly
overhead that some birds and
animals on the ground
never see the sun?

And there are insects
that look just
like leaves?

And trees start growing
high in the air
on top of other trees,
and send spindly roots down
to the ground?

179

Isn't it a wonder
that far up north
in the land of ice and snow
we call the arctic,

animals have winter coats
of fur as white as the snow?

Isn't it a wonder that some birds fly
thousands of miles over ocean and land . . .

and return to the same special spots,
to lay their eggs?

That salmon swim
hundreds of miles to shore
and far up the rivers
and over the waterfalls . . .

to return to the same special spots,
to lay their eggs?

Isn't it a wonder
that fireflies
have lights in their bodies
they can flash on and off . . .

that crickets "chirp" by rubbing
their wings?

That some fish
deep in the ocean
have little "electric lights"
dangling in front
of their noses as they swim?

LANTERNFISH

ANGLER

Or little lights
along their sides?

FIREFLY FISH

185

Isn't it a wonder
that out in the pond
smooth wiggly tadpoles
lose their tails
and grow legs,
and turn into frogs?

And that fuzzy caterpillars
weave silken cocoons
around themselves
and go to sleep,
then wake up as pretty moths
or butterflies?

Isn't it a wonder
that a little baby
that couldn't walk or talk
or feed itself . . .

should grow up to be you?

NOAH'S ARK

Long ago, when the world was new, there lived
a man named Noah.

Noah lived in peace and happiness with his
family. God saw this and was pleased. God also
saw that other people were selfish and cruel
to each other.

God said to Noah, "I am going to wash away the evil in the world with a great flood." He told Noah to build a special boat, called an ark, to save his family.

"Bring into the ark two of every kind of animal," God told Noah. "Gather plenty of food and store it on the ark for everyone."

Noah told his family what God had said to him. "We must obey God," said Noah.

Noah and his family began their work right away. Some people laughed when they saw Noah building a big boat so far away from water. But Noah trusted God.

Noah's family gathered lots of food to take on the ark—berries, fruits, vegetables, nuts. They stored hay for the horses, grain for the cattle, and meat for the lions and tigers.

Finally, the ark was ready! That's when God sent Noah two of every kind of animal in the world.

In marched the animals, two by two,
The long-necked giraffe and the kangaroo,
The walrus and the wallaby, too—
Up the ramp, two by two.
Up the ramp flipped two slippery seals,
And after them came two electric eels,
Badger and beaver, bear and gnu—
Up the ramp, two by two.

After Noah's family and the last pair of animals had stepped into the ark, the Lord shut them in. Some raindrops fell, *plink-plunk,* on the roof of the ark.

It began to rain harder, and then it poured!
The wind howled. The thunder roared. Lightning
flashed in jagged streaks across the sky.

Soon the ark began to float, and the water kept rising. After a while, even the mountain peaks disappeared from sight! It would rain for forty days and forty nights.

All life on earth was destroyed, but everyone in the ark was safe.

Noah and his family kept busy taking care of all the animals.

The animals grew uneasy. The wolves howled and the horses whinnied. Even the great striped tigers crouched in a corner and meowed like kittens.

Noah's family grew restless in the crowded, noisy ark. Had God forgotten them? Would it ever stop raining? But Noah trusted God. And finally, just as God had said it would, the rain stopped.

God made the sun shine and a warm wind blow. Little by little, the water went down.

One day, the ark lurched and bumped against the top of a mountain.

Noah wanted to know if there was dry land anywhere. He sent a raven out a window. Away it flew, up into the sunny sky. But soon it came back. There had been no place for it to land.

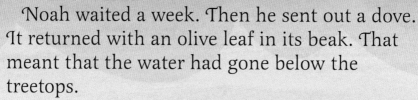

Noah waited a week. Then he sent out a dove. It returned with an olive leaf in its beak. That meant that the water had gone below the treetops.

Noah waited another week, then sent the dove out again. This time, the dove did not come back. That meant that the land was dry now, and the dove had found a place to live.

"Come out of the ark," God told Noah.

So Noah opened the door of the ark.
Fresh air rushed in. The people and the
animals felt warm sunlight on their faces.

The animals were so happy to be free! They pranced and hopped and waddled and slithered down the ramp onto dry land.

The bears ambled into the forests. The lions raced to the plains. The birds and monkeys hurried to the jungles. And some animals, the tame ones like the sheep and cattle, stayed close to Noah.

Noah's family was happy, too. They built an altar to God, and thanked God for keeping them safe. That's when God made a beautiful rainbow shine across the sky.

And God blessed Noah and his family, saying, "I will never again cover the earth with water. This rainbow is a sign of my promise to you. Whenever you see a rainbow, remember this promise."